Ellie's First Day

RiAnne Smith

illustrated by Yujie Studios

Dedicated to my family. Hugs ! I love you.

Thank you to Bearapy, Inc and Miss Kanisha Adams Barnes for the Young Authors Workshop scholarship.
Without your class, I might not have tried to write a book all by myself.

Thank you to Miss Danielle, my dance teacher at Dance Etc. who makes every class fun - especially with our "roll a tap move" games.

Thank you Daddy for supporting me and making sure this book looks like what I dreamed it would.

Thank you to my illustration team at Yujie Studios who drew the best Ellie!

To anyone who has ever wanted to dance —
Try your best, take a deep breathe and dance.
Never doubt yourself.
You've got this!

KEEPIN' UP WIT PRESS

Text copyright © 2022 RiAnne Smith

Printed in the USA

PB ISBN 978-1-953567-10-9
Library of Congress Control Number 2022913643

Ellie was excited to go to tap class. She got dressed in her leotard and put her tap shoes in her special dance bag. Ellie's mom did her hair in two buns. She added a blue headband.

Once Ellie was ready, Mom drove her to the dance studio for her first class.

When Ellie got to the studio, she was nervous. She saw many dancers. She listened to their tapping feet making beats on the floor.

"I don't know about this," Ellie said quietly.

Just then, the teacher looked at her.
"Hello! You must be Ellie," she said.
"I'm Miss Luna." Miss Luna smiled
at Ellie and bowed.

"Hi, Miss Luna," said Ellie.

Miss Luna took Ellie's hand and led her into the dance classroom.

"First, we need to stretch," she said.

Ellie stood in front of the big mirror and held the bar. Miss Luna showed Ellie how to stretch.

When it was time for class to start, Miss Luna clapped her hands.

"Come on, tappers!" she called.

Ellie wasn't nervous anymore. She was excited.

Miss Luna showed her students a step.
She tapped her toe on the floor, then
hopped on one foot.

"This is a pogo step," she explained.

Ellie laughed.

"You try it," Miss Luna said.
Ellie and her classmates tried
the step.

Next, Miss Luna swished her foot forward and back.
She stomped her foot. Then she stomped the other.
"Now try this step," said Miss Luna.

Ellie tried to shuffle ball change.
She was confused.

"I can't do it," she said.

Miss Luna came closer. She showed
Ellie the step slowly.

"Ready to try again?"
Miss Luna asked.
Ellie nodded.
She swished her foot on
the floor, then stomped
one foot after the other.

Ellie smiled. "I did it!"

"Yes, you did. Now let's try with music."
Miss Luna turned on the music, and
the students lined up to do the steps again.

The music was fast, and Ellie messed up her step. She stopped. She was sad.

Ruby, another student in the class, saw Ellie and came to stand next to her. "Watch me," she said. Ellie did.

"Let's try again," Ruby suggested.
Ellie did the step with Ruby.
"That's it!" Ruby told her.

Ellie began to smile. "I can do this," she said.

"You sure can," said Miss Luna.

"Ruby, thank you for helping."

Finally, the class was over. "Good job, everyone," Miss Luna said.

The class clapped. "Thank you,
Miss Luna," the students said together.

Ellie was happy. She skipped out of class.

Ellie couldn't wait to tell her mom all about the class. "Mom, it was great!" Ellie said. "I'm already learning tap steps and dancing!"

At home, Ellie stood on her bedroom floor barefoot. She looked in her mirror and tried the shuffle ball change and pogo step.

She remembered Miss Luna's instruction:

"Practice whenever you can, and you will be great!"

When it was time for the next class, Ellie checked her dance bag to make sure her tap shoes were ready. She put on her leotard, and Mom fixed her hair.

This time, Ellie was ready! She took her time with each new step, watching Miss Luna carefully.

Ellie smiled as she tapped.

"Let us dance!" Miss Luna said.

Ellie tapped.

And tapped.

And tapped.

meet the author

RiAnne Smith wrote this story when she was in second grade. She loves performing ballet and tap in her dance school's annual recital. She also likes to have fun and is always helping whoever needs her. RiAnne's imagination and her creativity know no limit.

She's proud to share Ellie's First Day, her first solo-authored book project.

CPSIA information can be obtained
at www.ICGtesting.com
Printed in the USA
LVHW072020211022
731268LV00009B/216